The Paper Princess

ELISA KLEVEN

PUFFIN BOOKS

To Donna and
to Susie, for her bravery

PUFFIN BOOKS
Published by the Penguin Group
Penguin Putnam Books for Young Readers, 345 Hudson Street,
New York, New York 10014, U.S.A.
Penguin Books Ltd, 80 Strand, London WC2R ORL, England
Penguin Books Australia Ltd, Ringwood, Victoria, Australia
Penguin Books Canada Ltd, 10 Alcorn Avenue, Toronto, Ontario, Canada M4V 3B2
Penguin Books (N.Z.) Ltd, 182-190 Wairau Road, Auckland 10, New Zealand
Penguin Books Ltd, Registered Offices: Harmondsworth, Middlesex, England

First published in the United States of America by Dutton Children's
Books, a division of Penguin Books USA Inc., 1994
Published in Puffin Books, 1998

9 10 8

Copyright © Elisa Kleven, 1994
All rights reserved

THE LIBRARY OF CONGRESS HAS CATALOGED THE DUTTON EDITION AS FOLLOWS:
Kleven, Elisa.
The paper princess/written and illustrated by Elisa Kleven.—1st ed.
p. cm.
Summary: A little girl makes a picture of a princess that comes to life
and is carried off by the wind.
ISBN 0-525-45231-1
[1. Drawing—Fiction. 2. Princesses—Fiction.] I. Title.
PZ7.K6783875Pap 1994
[E]—dc20 93-32612 CIP AC

Puffin Books ISBN 0-14-056424-1

Printed in the United States of America

A little girl sat in the sunshine, drawing a princess. The princess's dress was like a forest. Her socks were like starry skies. Her shoes were like watermelons. Her face was so friendly and brave that the little girl loved her.

What kind of hair should I give my princess? the little girl
wondered as she cut the princess out.

"Yarn hair would be soft," she said, offering the princess
a cracker.

Cotton hair would be fluffy, she thought, taking the princess for a ride.

WHOOSH! The wind sent the princess flying.

"Wait!" The girl chased after her. "I didn't finish you!"

"I'll finish myself!" the princess called in a voice as thin and new as she was.

"But I want to play with you!" the little girl cried. "You're the best thing I ever made. Don't blow away!"

The princess tried to fly back to the girl, but the wind carried her the other way. So she waved good-bye, then somersaulted through the air, over a meadow, over a river.

What kind of hair should I give myself? the princess wondered as she tumbled through the sky. Cloud hair is too cold, she thought, trying a little on.

"Blossom hair smells too sweet!" She sneezed.

"Candy-wrapper hair is too crinkly." She threw the candy wrapper off and sailed on, bald as the man in the moon…

arriving at a carnival. A boy on the Ferris wheel caught her. Hand in hand, they whirled around. The princess loved the ride, the colored lights, the stars, the jingling music, the warmth of the little boy's hand.

"Hello up there!" the boy's mother called. The boy waved
back, dropping the princess. The wind caught her up again.

It carried her into a town, past houses smelling of supper,
past children playing with dolls, past parents tucking their
children into bed. The princess saw them and felt homesick.

"I can do without hair," she said, "but I wish my little girl were with me." Gently, the wind rocked the princess until she drifted off to sleep. She floated like a leaf through the night.

The princess awoke to the sound of a little girl's voice. "What a pretty paper doll. Too bad they forgot to give it hair."

She didn't forget! the princess wanted to say. But the little girl's thumb was pressed over her mouth.

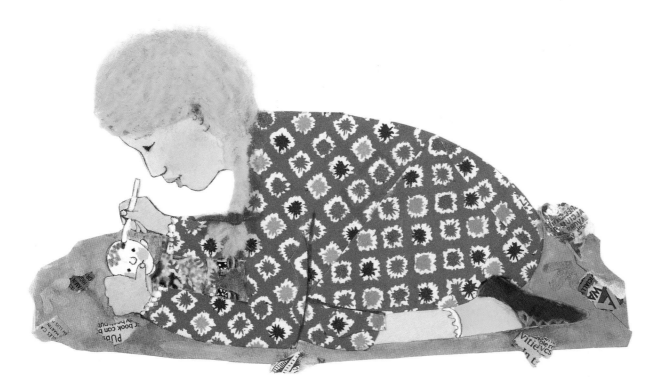

The girl took a pen out of her pocket, scribbled on the princess's head, and frowned. "Ugh," she said. "Green hair! I thought that was my yellow pen. Now it looks worse."

Before the princess could say a word, the girl crumpled her up and threw her into the garbage can.

The princess wanted to cry. Green hair is all right! she thought. She didn't have to crumple me!

"Help!" the princess tried to shout, but only a muffled squeak came out. She tried to jump out of the garbage can but was too tightly crumpled to move. Children came and went, throwing trash on top of her.

A jay came, pecking for food. "How lucky—a buttery bread crust!" the jay squawked. "How sweet—an apple core!" The jay pecked at the princess. "How handy—a fat wad of paper. I'll shred it to pieces and weave it into my nest."

"Bird, don't shred me!" the princess squeaked as the jay flew off with her. "Smooth me out so I can see the sun, and fly above the lovely world, and find the little girl who made me!"

What's this? the jay wondered, hearing the princess. Some little creature must be caught in this paper.

Back at her nest, the jay smoothed out the paper and saw the princess. "My gracious!" she cried. "Who are you?"

"I'm a princess," said the princess.

The jay brushed a speck of tuna fish from the princess's face. "Poor princess, all wrinkled with scribbled green hair. Let's cover it with something warm and soft."

She pulled a little real hair from her nest and stuck it onto the princess's head with sap.

"How pretty you look," the jay remarked as she brushed the princess's hair with a feather. "Is there anything else you would like?"

"I'd like to find the little girl who made me," said the princess.

"Where does she live?" asked the jay.

The princess tried to remember. "She lives near a tree with a swing, not far from a meadow, and a river, and a carnival. Do you think we can find her?"

"We can try," said the jay. "I'll carry you with my feet. Hold on tight!"

Away they flew, out past the town, over the carnival, over the river.

They saw many little girls, but they didn't see the one who made the princess.

At length, the jay stopped to rest. "I'm getting tired," she said, "and I'd better get back to my nest. Why don't you come home with me?"

"Thanks," replied the princess. "Thanks for everything you've done. But I'll keep looking for my little girl."

"Good luck," the jay said softly. She hugged the princess good-bye.

"I hope we meet again!" called the princess as the jay rose into the sky.

I hope I find my girl, she thought

as she fluttered

down to a meadow...

and landed beside a little boy. The boy's face was sweet but sad.

"What's the matter?" asked the princess.

"I drew a picture of the meadow, and it blew away," said the boy.

"Could you draw another picture like it?" asked the princess.

"I don't have any more paper," said the boy. "And it's getting dark."

The princess had an idea. "My other side is blank," she said. "You could draw on it."

"That wouldn't hurt you?" asked the boy.

"No," said the princess. "I'm paper. Just don't crumple me up if you don't like your picture."

"I won't," said the boy, and he began to draw.

"This picture is for my sister," the boy told the princess. "Today is her birthday."

"What's a birthday?" asked the princess.

"It's the day you were born," the boy explained, "the day you came into the world."

"My birthday was yesterday," the princess said. "A little girl drew me and cut me out. I want to get home to her."

"I'll help you find her. What does she look like?"

"She has brown hair and a friendly face," the princess said.

"My sister has brown hair," the boy replied. "And she's usually friendly."

"She fed me a cracker," the princess added. "And she loves to draw."

"My sister loves to draw," said the boy as he carried the princess home. "And I think she would love you."

He opened the door to his house. "Happy birthday!" he called to his sister, handing her the picture and the princess.

"What a beautiful picture!" his sister said. "But why is it shaped like—"

She turned the picture over. "My princess!" she cried. "It's you!" She gave the princess a kiss.

"It's *you!*" cried the princess, trembling with joy. "Happy birthday!"

"Where have you been?" asked the little girl. "Where did you find real hair?"

The princess told her story, about the search for hair, and the Ferris wheel, and the lonely night, and the scribble-girl, and the helpful jay, and the journey back to the brother in the meadow and home to the little girl.

While she listened, the girl made the princess a paper crown, and a cozy bed, and an elephant to ride, and a banjo to play, and a brother to play with, and a sweater to wear when she went out flying—

here, there, everywhere, and home again.

Other Picture Books
from Puffin